Dandelion Wishes

A Book of Modern-Day Fables

CHERI WOOD

Milli,
This is this because of you. I'm very grateful.

Love,
Cheri

Dandelion
Seed
Press

Copyright © 2017 Cheri Wood

Print edition

ISBN: 978-1-54391-516-7

Written by Cheri Wood
Interior illustrations © Cheri Wood
Cover illustration courtesy Shutterstock and Serg Dibrova
Cover design by Alchemy Book Cover Design
Dandelion Seed Press logo by Patricia Wilkinson
Author photo courtesy Danny Pendlebury

This is a work of fiction. Names, characters, places, and incidents are the product of the author's imagination. Any resemblance to actual persons, living or dead, businesses, companies, events, or locales is entirely coincidental.

Dandelion Seed Press
PO Box 230515
Encinitas, CA 92023

Author's website: cheriwood.com

Author's email address: author@cheriwood.com

For Laura

Table of Contents

"A children's story that can only be enjoyed by children is not a good children's story in the slightest."

—C.S. Lewis

Introduction

Dandelion Wishes started as bedtime storytelling when my daughter Laura was very young. I would make up stories on the fly every night, and usually each story had some sort of lesson or moral woven in as I would try to use characters and metaphor to turn everyday struggles and adventures into uplifting messages and teaching moments.

Sometimes I entertained the idea of writing down some of the stories, but I didn't get that far until Laura was old enough to go on overnight trips such as Girl Scout or YMCA camps. I began writing one story for every night she'd be away. I put each one in a dated envelope and sent it in her suitcase. Similarly, I would leave a story in an envelope on her dresser when I was traveling.

As Laura grew older, she attended a school that included a two-week residential summer program. I emailed fourteen stories to Laura, one each night, that first summer. This was my way of ensuring that Laura never missed having a bedtime story from me when she was still young enough to want them.

One day I noticed the printed stories opened and spread across Laura's bed. She'd saved them all and was re-reading them. I was touched, and it gave me the idea to create a hardcover book with illustrations for her. I had one copy printed as a gift. I titled it *Stories for Your Heart Whenever We're Apart* because that was precisely why I wrote the stories.

When she received the hardcover book, Laura said, "I want you to publish these so other kids will be able to read them." I hesitated for quite some time because the stories were for Laura, but then it occurred to me that the stories are hers and she wanted to share them. Turning some of the stories I wrote for Laura into a book to be published for a wider audience became my next labor of love.

Whether you're a parent reading stories to your children or a child who loves to read, I hope you enjoy *Dandelion Wishes* as much as I've enjoyed creating these stories for Laura.

Cheri Wood
San Diego, 2017

A Dandy Time

A WARM BREEZE BLEW across the meadow. Fluffy and Turbo felt themselves lifted and carried away. They floated on the warm breeze, much like a pair of sea turtles flowing along the Gulf Stream.

"Wheeeee!" shouted Fluffy.

"Whooooooaaaaaa!" wailed Turbo.

"What's the matter?" asked Fluffy.

"I'm afraid of going fast!" screamed Turbo.

"This is what we were born to do!" yelled Fluffy. "It's our destiny! Enjoy the ride!"

"Aaaaaaaaaaahhhhh!" cried Turbo.

As Fluffy and Turbo floated along, they tried to grab each other's tiny parachutes so they could travel together. That didn't work, but thank goodness they were headed in the same direction. The best they could hope for was to land near each other in full sunlight.

"On top of being afraid of traveling at such a speed," Turbo moaned, "I'm terribly sad!"

"Why?" Fluffy queried.

"Because," Turbo lamented, "I wanted my lift-off to be when someone made a special wish, not because of a random breeze."

"Oh, Turbo," Fluffy countered. "What does it matter how we got our start, so long as we get to be beautiful dandelions?"

"I guess you're right," said Turbo.

Just then the breeze picked up. Fluffy and Turbo tumbled about and were separated, one sailing way above the other. After a few moments, they managed to get side by side again.

"Isn't being *wished upon* a seed head's purpose in life?" questioned Turbo.

"I suppose many seed heads are wished upon, but not all," reasoned Fluffy, as she soared ahead of Turbo. "What about all the other seed heads that aren't wished upon? Do you think they're useless?"

"No," said Turbo. "I guess not."

Turbo tried to keep up with Fluffy, but she slipped even farther ahead.

"Of course they aren't useless," Fluffy said wisely. "However, it may be that when the individual seeds are set free, they go on to become lovely dandelions just the same—as soon as they land in decent soil, get a little water, and find the sun!"

Turbo caught up to Fluffy again. He was just starting to enjoy the ride when suddenly he felt himself drifting closer and closer to the ground. He looked to his left and right but didn't see Fluffy anywhere. He shifted over to one side to try to catch the breeze just so.

It worked! Turbo was up and floating again. The best part was that he could see Fluffy just up ahead. "Fluffy!" shouted Turbo.

Fluffy straightened herself out in order to slow down. Turbo caught up to her.

"Hey," said Turbo. "I'm really getting the hang of this floating business!"

A short while later Turbo and Fluffy felt themselves dropping down toward a warm grassy field. Nestling themselves into the soil just below the grass, they enjoyed the feel of the warm sun on their parachutes.

"This is a dandy place for us to grow," said Fluffy.

"I couldn't agree more," said Turbo. Then he added thoughtfully, "The next time we turn into seed heads, I'm really going to enjoy the ride!"

"I know you will," said Fluffy as she drifted off to sleep.

Turbo fell asleep shortly thereafter. They both needed some rest before their adventure could continue.

The Clumps

ONCE UPON A TIME, in a dark corner of a very large forest, there grew a family of mushrooms. There, near the root of a very old tree, was the home of The Clump Family.

The Clumps were not the most popular family in the forest. They had a musky scent that some people did not find appealing. Their appearance was also off-putting to certain folk because they were a little soiled most of the time, owing to their dirty home at the root of that old tree.

Now Papa Clump was a hearty old soul, and he very much liked to tell a story to anyone who would listen. Papa Clump's stories were said to be his own true adventures, but everyone knew they were peppered with just enough fantasy to spice them up just right.

Since his wife, Mama Clump, and their three children, Porcini, Shiitake, and Portobello—who was nicknamed Bello, for short—were never far away, Papa Clump had the perfect audience for his storytelling.

One night, as Porcini, Shiitake and Bello were falling asleep, Papa Clump told this story:

There I was, just a wee button of a mushroom in my youth, when I heard them coming! It was before Mama Clump and you little Clump children started growing nearby. Alone I was, just me and the old tree.

I looked up and saw Owl, the one who hoots us to sleep some nights, but the feathered coward sat still as a stone. He'd be no help.

I tried to nestle deeper into the soil and hoped they would walk right by. But, as luck would have it, they stopped to sit under the tree. There were two of them, and no sooner did they sit down to open their picnic basket than I was spotted.

"Oh!" said the female one. "Look at that lovely mushroom! Don't you think it would be delicious in a breakfast omelet?"

"Don't touch it!" said the male picnicker.

"Why?" asked the woman, who had a very kind voice, by the way.

"Because it's just a toadstool!" said the man. "They're poisonous."

Now, I don't mind telling you that I was mighty insulted. I thought for a moment of telling that man what a big mistake he'd made thinking I was a poisonous toadstool. But then I remembered what your Granny Clump taught me. She used to say, "Pride cometh before a fall."

So I let those two picnickers go right on thinking whatever they wanted to think about me. I knew who I was, and if those two couldn't recognize my value as a mushroom, well, that was their loss. "I'd rather be happy and alive than eaten for the wrong reason!"

As Mama Clump fluffed up the soil around Porcini, Shiitake, and Bello, they drifted off to sleep, dreaming of toadstools and picnics. Papa Clump was very pleased with his storytelling that night.

Bear Necessities

ONCE UPON A TIME there were three bears.

Now, these bears weren't the ones from the story about Goldilocks. No way. These three bears were teenagers and they hardly had any hair.

In fact, one of them was so bald he practically looked human. So human that he was able to get away with going to the movies. Most people thought he was just a homely-looking boy so they paid very little attention to him. Besides movies, this bear was also quite fond of parties and was able to sneak into birthday celebrations at Chuck E. Cheese.

The bear and his two friends realized that if he could easily walk into the movies or Chuck E. Cheese he might as well go into Target and buy them some hair removal cream. They were getting a little tired of having to cram themselves around the iPad to watch Netflix. With a couple of bottles of a good depilatory, the other two bears would be able to pass themselves off as humans and go see a movie with their friend.

It took a while to get up his nerve, but the "boy bear" was able to get two bottles of hair remover. With the coupons his mother clipped from the newspaper, the bears even had enough money left over to get one apple each at Whole Foods.

It was there that the trouble began.

"AHHHHHH!" screamed one of the cashiers upon noticing three bald bears entering the store.

The manager came running out from the storeroom where he'd been husking corn for the summer shoppers.

"What is it?" he demanded, looking around.

"There!" The cashier pointed dramatically. "Bears! In the market!"

"Now, now," the manager scolded. "Those boys may be a tad unattractive, but let's not insult our paying customers."

The three bears tried very hard not to giggle. They walked boldly into the produce section to select their apples.

One picked a Granny Smith.

One picked a Fuji.

And the first bear, who was so fond of parties? He picked a Gala, of course.

Polly Wants a Quacker

So, OF COURSE, the most delicious treat to have with tomato soup is a cracker. Just ask Polly.

One day, while Polly's mother was at work, Polly decided to make herself some tomato soup.

Just as Polly began warming up the soup, the phone rang.

"Hello?" said Polly.

"Oh, hello, dear," said Polly's mother. "I just wanted to remind you we're out of saltines. Maybe you should make yourself a nice peanut butter sandwich instead of soup."

"But, Mother!" said Polly. "I'm already making tomato soup. It's in the pot and everything."

"I'm sorry, dear," said Polly's mother. "Perhaps you should go to the market for crackers."

A funny thing happened on the way to the store to buy saltines.

Polly was riding her bike down the street when she noticed a family of ducks waddling across the pavement. It was a mother and her six ducklings. One duckling, the last in line, stopped to check out every butterfly, flower, blade of grass, and stone on the path along the way. He was very distracted and pretty soon he was left behind.

Polly thought he was the most adorable little duckling she'd ever seen.

"Hey, little duckie," said Polly. "What's your name?"

"Quacker," said the duckling.

"What a cute name!" said Polly. "Well, Quacker, you'd best hurry and catch up to the other ducks."

"Oh, they'll come back and get me," said Quacker. "They always do. I'll just wait right here."

"Are you sure?" asked Polly.

"Oh, yes," said the duckling. "Mother always says: *The next time you get lost, be sure to wait in the very last place we saw each other!*"

Hearing that the duckling had a plan, Polly started off down the road on her bike. She was really hungry for her tomato soup and crackers. But, as she pedaled off, she could not stop thinking about that little duckling alone on the side of the road.

Polly turned her bike around and went back to find the duckling. She would sit with him until his mother and brothers and sisters came back for him. Polly had decided she liked Quacker much more than crackers anyway.

It Was a Dark and Stormy Knight

NOBODY COULD UNDERSTAND why Percival was such a cranky knight. It seemed he had everything he could ever want. He lived in a palace. He could go swimming in the moat—which did not have alligators—any time he wanted. He had a strong white horse to ride. He had a pet monkey to play with him. Percival had all of the best toys in the kingdom.

None of these things made Percival happy deep down inside, but Percival didn't know why. All he knew was that he felt cranky.

One day when Percival rode his horse into town, he stopped off at the local tailor's shop to see about getting a new suit. Whenever he wasn't wearing a suit of armor he always made sure he wore the latest fashionable clothing. But when he got there the tailor's shop was closed. This made Percival cranky, so he went to the coffee shop next door to get some tea.

It was there, in the coffee shop, at a small table by the window, that he spotted a lovely girl.

Now, Percival was very shy. Because when a person is very cranky he won't have many friends, and when someone doesn't have many friends, he may become shy.

Percival ordered at the counter. While he waited for his tea, he kept sneaking peeks at the pretty girl. Then Percival looked for a table where he could sit and gaze upon the girl while he drank his tea, but all the tables were occupied.

Of course, no one invited Percival to sit down. He was so disagreeable the townsfolk had gotten used to avoiding him. He stood there with his cup of tea and nowhere to sit.

Feeling unhappy, Percival went outside. He stood on the sidewalk, drank his tea quickly, burned his tongue, and felt even crankier than usual.

As he mounted his horse to ride away, the girl at the small table by the window looked out at Percival. She gazed at his face and whispered to herself, "How handsome that young knight would be if only he would smile."

As Percival rode off into the distance, he thought about the pretty girl by the window. Despite his burned tongue and nobody offering him a seat in the coffee shop and riding all the way to town for a new suit he couldn't buy, the thought of her made him break into a smile!

The girl couldn't see his smile, only his stiff back and shoulders as he sat upon his horse.

Every day for the next week, Percival thought about her and smiled. He noticed that he liked the feeling a smile makes. He started testing his smile in front of other people.

Soon enough the townsfolk noticed the change in Percival's demeanor. They started smiling back at him and this made Percival's smile grow even bigger. Now he was spending more and more time in town, chatting and even laughing with his new friends.

This made Percival happy deep down inside.

One day in the crowded coffee shop, Percival smiled at the man behind the counter. Just after he ordered his tea, someone with a sweet voice called out across the crowd, inviting him to sit down. It was the pretty girl at the table by the window.

If It's Not One Thing, It's Your Mother

A SENSIBLE GIRL NAMED Sally Ann lived on a farm with lots of animals, including three horses. One was a filly named Whinny. The other two were Whinny's mother and father, Mr. & Mrs. Gallup. The three horses lived together in a barn.

Sally Ann's parents kept a small black-and-white TV out in the barn. The horses could see the TV screen from their stalls. Sally Ann loved watching *Jeopardy* in the barn. She loved knowing her favorite horses were standing nearby eating their hay while she watched her favorite show.

Whinny and Mr. & Mrs. Gallup loved watching *Jeopardy* with Sally Ann. The horses had a great time shouting out the answers in horse talk. They would get so excited about playing the game, they were even louder than the audience clapping and cheering on the show.

Sometimes Sally Ann couldn't hear parts of the show because of the hoof-stamping and neighing coming from the stalls!

However, in *Final Jeopardy* the horses had agreed to wait until the music stopped before they shared their guesses.

In the early evening the farm was a peaceful place. Cows mooed in the pasture as they grazed. Chickens pecked at their corn or sat on their eggs. Pigs wiggled in the mud. Sheep snoozed on the grassy knoll. A kitten batted at a butterfly with her front paw, but not hard enough to hurt its wings.

One evening, just as *Final Jeopardy* was about to finish, Sally Ann heard a particularly pointed neigh coming from Mrs. Gallup. Her filly Whinny neighed right back.

"Don't shout out the answer!" said Mrs. Gallup.

"I didn't mean to!" shouted Whinny. "I got too excited!"

But it was all in horse talk.

Sally Ann walked over to Whinny's stall and said, "If I didn't know any better, I'd say you just got scolded by your mother!"

Whinny just looked at Sally Ann with her big brown eyes, and then she nodded her head, like horses do. Sally Ann took the nod to mean that Whinny wanted an apple.

Holding out an apple, Sally Ann said, "Whinny, do you want this apple?"

Whinny nodded her head again, like horses do. Sally Ann gave Whinny the apple.

"Whinny, I do think you got scolded," said Sally Ann, watching Whinny's cheek bulge as she munched the apple. "I recognize the tone in your mother's voice, even if it was a neigh. It's the same tone my mother takes with me when she wants me to behave myself."

Whinny blinked her long black lashes.

Sally Ann said, "Whinny, you must listen to your mother. Now behave yourself. Your mother is just looking out for you, as mothers do."

Mollie & Culey

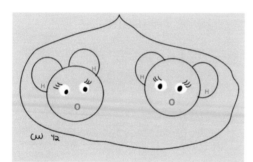

ONCE UPON A TIME there was a beautiful land called Dewdrop. In it were tiny little beings. Two of the tiny beings in Dewdrop were named Mollie and Culey.

Mollie and Culey had a close bond and went everywhere together. They really enjoyed dancing together on blades of grass in the early morning hours of a summer day. Sometimes they would hang out at the end of a leaf on a tree, and it really gave them a charge to see how long they could stay there before dropping to the ground.

One of their favorite activities was clinging to a spider web while the spider was away. And the most exciting thing of all? A wild ride on the roof of a car after a night of condensation.

But Mollie and Culey wanted to see what else was out in the world to explore. Dewdrop would appear most mornings. It was the same old thing day after day, week after week, season after season. They decided to make their escape from the land of Dewdrop.

There they were, sitting in the grass, thinking about what to do. Leaving Dewdrop was against the rules until a certain age, but Mollie and Culey thought that if they just left for *a little while*, they wouldn't get caught.

On that fine summer morning, they set out on their adventure—or so they tried. Each time they got to the edge of Dewdrop it was like looking through a window. They couldn't get through.

Just then a beautiful butterfly landed right next to them. She looked into Dewdrop just as Mollie and Culey looked out.

"Hi," said the butterfly. "What are your names?"

"Mollie and Culey," they answered in unison. "What's yours?"

"My name is Buttercup," said the butterfly.

"We want to get out of here," said Mollie and Culey. "Can you help us?"

"Hmm. . . ." said Buttercup. "I have an idea."

Buttercup stuck out her straw-like tongue and took a careful sip from Dewdrop, sucking Mollie and Culey gently into her proboscis. She carried them over to a lovely flower in a bed near the grass where she gently let the sip bits out of her mouth.

Mollie and Culey came tumbling out! Right away they found themselves being pulled toward a large drop of water—it was larger than the land of Dewdrop! They began to cry and call out to their new friend.

"Oh, Buttercup! We're being pulled by some strange force toward the big drop next to us! Please help!"

Buttercup thought fast, but not fast enough.

She stuck out her tongue to try to grab the two friends, but they had already moved into Big Drop. Even worse, it looked like a huge bumblebee was about to land and take a drink of Big Drop!

Buttercup thought fast again. She decided to risk making the bumblebee angry. She poked around and around inside Big Drop until she found Mollie and Culey. Gently she took them into her proboscis—and not a moment too soon!

As the bumblebee drank from Big Drop, Buttercup carried them home as fast as her wings could flutter.

But it was too late. Dewdrop was gone! It had disappeared with the late morning sun, as it always did.

Mollie and Culey were bereft. They had been so tired of the same old routine at Dewdrop and now they would give anything to be there!

Buttercup had nowhere else to take them, so after the bumblebee was gone she put Mollie and Culey back down in what was left of Big Drop.

"I hope you find your way home!" she said.

As the sun warmed and took Big Drop away for the day, Mollie and

Culey held onto each other tightly.

The next morning Mollie and Culey woke up. They looked around and realized they were safe in Dewdrop where they belonged.

"Did we have a bad dream?" asked Mollie.

"I don't know," said Culey. "It felt so real."

"Let's never, ever break the rules and leave Dewdrop, okay?" said Mollie and Culey in unison.

"I want to stay safe in Dewdrop until we learn more about the world and can join a lovely pond," Mollie added.

"Or maybe a cloud," proposed Culey.

"Or maybe a babbling brook," said Mollie.

"We have so much time to experience things and grow before we decide," they said in unison.

"Hey, I know," said Culey. "Let's watch for Buttercup today and ask her if she's ever been to a pond or seen a cloud or had a drink from a babbling brook."

"Great idea!" said Mollie.

From that day forward, Mollie and Culey lived happily in the land of Dewdrop. Buttercup stayed close to her new friends so she could tell them stories and protect them until they were grown up and ready to leave home.

Lazuli & Gerbera

ONCE UPON A TIME there was a beautiful Blue Morpho butterfly named Lazuli. Her wings were as blue as the lapis lazuli, a smooth, pretty gemstone of the deepest blue you can imagine.

Lazuli found herself fluttering about one bright summer morning. The breeze grew warmer as noon approached. The colors in the lush gardens and meadows below her were all so tempting. She began searching for a flower from which she could take a sip of something delicious.

"Which flower shall I choose?" Lazuli asked herself aloud.

"Oh, pick me!" said Gerbera, a lovely orange daisy nestled with her yellow, red, pink and white sisters in a fragrant meadow.

"I think I shall!" declared Lazuli. "Never have I seen such a lovely daisy in all of my flutterings!" Lazuli landed on Gerbera's petals. They began to chat and immediately became close friends.

Soon Lazuli was going to the meadow every morning to land on Gerbera's soft petals and chat. Gerbera looked forward to Lazuli's wings tickling her petals and making her giggle.

One night it began to rain. Soon the rain turned to hail. There was thunder and lightning. The rain lasted all of the next day. Lazuli was worried that Gerbera's soft petals would be bruised in the hail—or worse.

"What if the soil becomes too soft and soggy from rainwater?" Lazuli asked her mother. "And what if Gerbera's roots can no longer hold on?"

"Don't worry, Lazuli," her mother said. "Mother Nature will take care of Gerbera and her sisters."

The rain continued for a second night. The thunder and lightning made Lazuli feel like crying, but she tried to be very brave. Finally, she fell asleep from pure exhaustion.

The next morning Lazuli awoke and heard birds chirping. The rain had stopped! She stretched her beautiful blue wings and fluttered up into the sky. Lazuli never fluttered faster as she headed straight for the meadow.

Everywhere she looked the colors seemed brighter than ever. The sky was blue. The clouds were puffy and white. The grass below her was lush and green. Every leaf on every tree practically sparkled in shades of green and yellow.

And then something orange caught Lazuli's attention. There she was! Gerbera waved her petals in the warm summer breeze, just like the day they first met.

Lazuli fluttered down and landed on Gerbera's soft petals. Gerbera giggled at the tickling of Lazuli's wings. The friends had so much to talk about!

Good Scents

IT SEEMED TO FREDERICA that she would never get there. She walked and walked and walked, but every time she turned a corner or got to the top of an incline, there was only more road ahead.

Sammy was her new friend and at least they could walk together. It was a good thing, too, because nobody else wanted to walk with them. Frederica and Sammy didn't know why.

"Do you think it's our black-and-white outfits?" asked Sammy.

"I don't think so," said Frederica. "I think our black tails and the white stripes down our backs are especially cute today!"

Frederica and Sammy kept walking. It was hot. They were hungry. And Frederica's feet were killing her.

"Oh, Sammy," said Frederica. "Why don't your feet hurt as much as mine?"

"I think they might," said Sammy. "But there isn't anything I can do about it, so I just deal with it."

Just when it seemed to Frederica that they might have to walk for the rest of their lives, she spied shady trees and picnic tables up ahead.

"Hallelujah!" shouted Frederica.

"We made it!" said Sammy excitedly.

As soon as the girls put down their lunch bags at the lovely wooden picnic table, everyone sitting there got up and moved to another table.

Sammy got tears in her eyes. Frederica said, "I've had enough of this. I want to know what's up!"

Sammy said, "Oh, Frederica, let's just forget about it and eat by ourselves."

"No," said Frederica. "I want to get to the bottom of this!"

Sammy smiled.

"Why are you smiling?" asked Frederica.

"Because," Sammy said, with her grin getting bigger, "I just realized that to find out what's up you have to get to the bottom of it."

Frederica and Sammy laughed and laughed. In fact, they got the giggles so hard they began to roll around in the grass by the picnic table.

A little creature in brown fur with a lovely curled and bushy tail was munching on nuts by a tree. She stopped munching and approached

Frederica and Sammy.

"Hi, my name is Carmelina. Why are you two laughing so hard?"

"It's kind of an inside joke," Frederica said. "We'd love to let you in on it."

"I'd like that," said Carmelina. "But I have to go back to my friends now. They didn't want to come over here because, well, you know."

"No," said Frederica, with her smile fading. "We don't know what you mean."

Sammy said, "Yeah, that's what the joke was about. We want to 'get to the bottom of what's up' with everyone who won't come near us!"

Carmelina giggled and said, "Get to the bottom of what's up? Ha-hahahaha! That *is* funny! Now I understand why you were laughing so hard."

"Okaaaaay," said Frederica. "But why does everyone stay away from us?"

Carmelina cleared her throat. She paused. She blinked. And then she stammered, "Well, I thought you knew. I guess, I mean, well, it's because of the, um, let's see, well, um, the . . . *aroma* coming from you, which I guess you can't help."

Frederica and Sammy started giggling again. Carmelina breathed a sigh of relief.

"You aren't mad?" asked Carmelina.

"Of course not!" said Frederica. "You see, whenever we get nervous or frightened we make that smell. And today Sammy and I were very nervous about being the new girls."

"We have never been to this forest or met you before," Sammy added, "so we didn't realize that you weren't used to our smell."

Carmelina understood. "Well, you don't have to be nervous here," she assured her new friends. "We may not all come from the same place or look alike, but we can all be very good friends."

And so, as Frederica and Sammy rested and felt less nervous and smelled better, everyone gathered around to introduce themselves to the two new girls.

A Little Bit of Courage

I<small>T WAS A BEAUTIFUL DAY</small> in the small town of Haymarket. Chloe was on her pony riding over to Raquel's house when she heard a strange noise coming from the pasture. She tied her pony to the fence, right next to the mailbox, and went to investigate.

Two cows named Bessie and Trulie were standing still, chewing their cud, and blinking their eyes in the sunshine. Chloe looked around and saw nothing amiss when again she heard a strange noise. It seemed to be coming from the tree at the end of the meadow near a stream.

While the cows minded their own business Chloe walked over to the tree. Something caught her attention in the branches and she looked up.

It was a tiny kitten stuck in the tree!

"I wonder how she got way up there," Chloe thought.

Luckily she was wearing long pants and she quickly climbed up into the tree. When Chloe reached the branch with the kitten, it nuzzled up to her arm and purred.

"Don't worry," she said. "I will help you get down."

"MEOW!" said the kitten with all of its might.

"What's wrong?" asked Chloe. "Do you want to stay in the tree?"

The kitten relaxed and starting purring. Chloe picked up the kitten and began to climb down.

"MEOW!" said the kitten and held tight with her claws.

"Ouch!" cried Chloe. "You're scratching me. Are you scared?"

The kitten rubbed its head on Chloe's arm and seemed to be saying "YES!"

Chloe sat with the kitten in the tree for a bit. She wondered if her friend Raquel would still be waiting for her. They had planned to go get their favorite Jamba Juice smoothie that day, and Chloe was hoping Raquel wouldn't leave without her.

While Chloe sat and thought about Jamba Juice, she watched the cows below her nosing around for some juicy grass to munch. Bessie and Trulie moved closer to the tree where the grass was longer.

"MEOW!" said the kitten with all of its might.

"Ohhh, is that the trouble?" Chloe asked. "You're afraid of the cows?"

The kitten snuggled itself tightly next to Chloe. "Meow, meow!"

"I promise those cows won't bother you," said Chloe. "In fact, if you can be very brave and trust me, I think you'll find out that cows are wonderful, especially for little kittens."

The kitten looked doubtful and gave a little shiver.

"If you stay up in the tree," Chloe explained, "you'll miss out on adventures and fun, that's for sure. Sometimes it can be a little scary to take a risk, but often the best rewards come after courage is shown."

For such a little kitten she was wise and trusting and brave. Chloe encouraged her to climb down from the tree all by herself. Chloe followed the tiny kitten, branch by branch.

When Chloe and the kitten were at the trunk of the tree, Chloe said, "Come on, little kitten, I will introduce you to Bessie and Trulie."

The kitten meowed and gave another little shiver—and then she walked right up to the cows.

"Bessie and Trulie," said Chloe. "I'd like you to meet this little kitten."

"Mooo!" said Bessie and Trulie warmly.

"And now," said Chloe, "let's give the kitten a treat!"

Chloe knelt down by Bessie and took an udder into her hand. She squeezed out a little milk and squirted it in the direction of the kitten. The kitten opened her tiny pink mouth just as the warm milk sprayed her. She licked her whiskers. It was delicious!

Chloe sprayed a few more squirts into the kitten's mouth, first from

Bessie and then from Trulie. The kitten had been so thirsty! The milk was so sweet and good!

"I'm so glad you were courageous and tried something new!" Chloe said to the kitten. "Isn't it wonderful? I'm going to name you Little Bit."

Little Bit purred with delight.

"Goodbye, Little Bit," said Chloe. "You're little but you're brave. I think you'll be just fine now."

She walked to the fence, untied her pony, and rode as fast as she could to Raquel's house. She couldn't wait to tell Raquel about the courageous little kitten that climbed out of the tree all by herself.

Spot On

"I'M SO TIRED of this red-and-black spotted jacket!" a tiny little ladybug exclaimed one day. She was ready for a new outfit. The ladybug flitted into the thrift store on the corner.

"May I help you?" asked the butterfly behind the counter.

The tiny little ladybug thanked her and said she'd like to just take a look around.

"Suit yourself," said the butterfly.

"Hmm," thought the tiny little ladybug with mirth. "That's exactly what I want to do!"

The first outfit she saw on a hanger near the door was fuzzy yellow with black stripes. She tried it on, but it was kind of sticky.

"That one belonged to a honeybee," said the butterfly.

"Oh," said the tiny little ladybug.

The next outfit she tried on was feathered and a lovely shade of blue.

"That one belonged to a blue jay," said the butterfly.

"It's a little big for me," said the tiny little ladybug.

"You could have it tailored," said the butterfly.

"I think I'll keep looking," said the tiny little ladybug. "Ta-ta for now!"

"Stop by again!" said the butterfly.

The tiny little ladybug flitted out of the thrift store and went all the way across town. She flitted her way into an upscale department store. She tried on a fuzzy brown spider outfit, but it had way too many arms and legs. She tried on a roly-poly bug outfit. Although it was very sleek, it felt like wearing a suit of armor.

Discouraged, the tiny little ladybug decided to go visit the zoo. A day visiting with many different animals always cheered her right up.

First the tiny little ladybug flitted over to the elephants, then to the zebras, and then over to watch the giraffes eating eucalyptus leaves from tall branches.

Finally, she came near the leopard enclosure. The leopards were all sleeping, except for one tiny little leopard playing near her mother. The tiny little ladybug and the tiny little leopard began chatting about this and that.

"What have you been doing today?" asked the tiny little leopard.

"Oh, I've been out shopping," said the tiny little ladybug.

"What for?" asked the tiny little leopard.

"I want a new outfit," said the tiny little ladybug. "But I've given up trying. I couldn't find anything that looked or felt just right. Now I'm feeling discouraged about wearing this same old red-and-black spotted jacket for the rest of my life!"

"Why would you want to change your outfit," asked the tiny little leopard, "when the one you have suits you so perfectly?"

"Because I think there may be a more beautiful outfit somewhere," said the tiny little ladybug. "If there is one, I want to be sure I don't miss it."

The tiny little leopard looked confused. "But your outfit is a tiny little ladybug outfit, isn't it?"

"Of course," the tiny little ladybug replied.

"Well, then, aren't you already wearing a perfectly wonderful outfit?" asked the tiny little leopard. And then she added, "I think you'd look like *someone else* if you wore something else. Don't you just want to be yourself?"

The tiny little ladybug thought about this. It made sense.

The tiny little ladybug and the tiny little leopard continued chatting about this and that.

"Have you ever thought about changing your outfit?" asked the tiny little ladybug.

"Oh, no," responded the tiny little leopard.

"Why not?" asked the tiny little ladybug.

"A leopard never changes her spots!" explained the tiny little leopard.

"You know what?" the tiny little ladybug said to the tiny little leopard.

"What?" questioned the tiny little leopard.

"I've been spending quite a bit of time looking around to see if there was something better for me to wear. I was busy doing that instead of appreciating my perfectly lovely red-and-black spotted jacket. You're right. This outfit really is sooo me!"

"Your logic is spot on!" said the tiny little leopard.

And then the tiny little ladybug and the tiny little leopard giggled so hard their spots wiggled.

Justice and Cupcakes Served

IN THE INTEREST of serving justice, a group of young fairies set up shop on Krandolia Boulevard in the village of Ossatera. They called themselves the Honorable Fairies of Fairness and Decision.

It seemed to these fairies there was always some dispute or disagreement going on in the village. They felt someone ought to do something about it—so they did.

They were fortunate to find an abandoned storefront that would suit their needs perfectly. Inside the shop they painted the walls a pale yellow color and washed the stone floors until they shone. They set up a long wooden table and placed five chairs behind the table facing out into the room. They filled the rest of the room with benches upon which people with disputes and disagreements could sit.

Next they hung out their shingle, which read, "Fairy Court of Fairness and Decision," of course. The nameplates in front of each chair read as follows:

The Honorable Tammy

The Honorable Dolly

The Honorable Loretta

The Honorable Patsy

　　and

The Honorable Kitty

Soon the Fairy Court was open for business.

On the very first day two sisters were seen in front of the baker's shop on Krandolia Boulevard fighting over the wand they shared. The baker stepped outside to see what all the fuss was about.

"I polished the wand yesterday!" said one sister. "Now it's her turn."

"No!" said the second sister. "I'm the one who polished it yesterday!"

The baker held up his hand.

"Stop!" he said. "This is clearly a matter for the Fairy Court of Fairness and Decision."

He quickly sent the two sisters down the street to meet the fairy judges. Tammy, Dolly, Loretta, Patsy and Kitty were pleased to have their very first case.

So many village people came to court that day the local police officer had to ask a couple of his friends (one was a construction worker and one was a sailor) to help with the crowd. Pretty soon the courtroom crowd spilled out onto the sidewalk. Seeing this, the construction worker and the sailor asked two of their friends (one was a motorcycle rider and one was a Native American chief) to help out.

As soon as everyone inside got settled on the benches in Fairy Court and the village people standing on the sidewalk were quiet, the five fairies called the court to order. The Honorable Tammy called the first case—the two sisters and the matter of the dirty wand—to come forward.

Within moments the sisters began to argue about the wand. They sounded like a broken record.

"I polished the wand yesterday!" said the first sister. "Now it's her turn."

"No!" said the second sister. "I'm the one who polished it yesterday!"

The Honorable Tammy had to clear her throat. When that didn't work, she firmly tapped her own wand on the wooden table several times to bring order to the court.

Tap, tap, tap!

The sisters became quiet.

"Now," said the Honorable Dolly. "We'll pretend that the wand is a talking stick. Whoever is holding it may speak, but she must never talk about her sister, only about herself. Then she must pass the talking stick to her sister, who must do the same."

The sister holding the wand that was now the talking stick said, "Every time it's her turn, my sister always tries to get away with—"

"Halt!" said the Honorable Loretta.

"You must only talk about yourself," said the Honorable Patsy.

"Um, I believe I polished the wand yesterday," said the first sister, as she shoved the talking stick toward her sister.

The second sister grabbed the talking stick and quickly replied, "You are wrong and must be lazy because—"

"Cease!" said the Honorable Kitty.

"Oops," said the second sister. "I believe I polished the wand yesterday after we came back from the beach."

She handed the talking stick back to her sister.

"Um, well," the first sister stuttered. "I can say that I had a really fun time at the beach with you."

She passed the talking stick over.

"Yes, uh, it was such a beautiful day!" said the second sister. "I was so tired when we got back."

She passed back the talking stick to her sibling.

"Yes, it was a wonderful day in every way," said the first sister. "I, too, was very tired and so I took a nap the minute we came home."

Back went the talking stick to the second sister.

"I polished the wand while you were napping," said the second sister. She smiled and added, "I guess that's why you didn't know it had been polished."

She gave her sister the talking stick.

The first sister said, "I thought the wand looked awfully shiny when I woke up!"

Both sisters were smiling now. "The wand has indeed been polished!" they said in unison.

The first sister looked at the second sister. "I guess it's my turn to polish the wand!"

The sisters hugged and the courtroom cheered. The five fairy judges had resolved their first case.

"We've done a great job settling disputes and disagreements on our very first day!" the fairies said in unison.

They closed up shop early and bought five chocolate cupcakes from the baker to celebrate.

Old Dogs, New Things

"WHAT IS ALL that racket?" grumbled Dagney to himself.

Dagney was an old hound dog who lived in the Gundersens' backyard. Candie Gundersen loved the old hound dog, even if he was rather sullen and less playful than he used to be when they were both much younger. Candie was eleven, and so was Dagney—but there's a big difference between human and dog years, so Dagney wasn't nearly as spry as Candie these days.

Candie came out the back door and ran into the yard barefoot. Her hair was in two pigtails, but she hadn't put on her shoes yet. Dagney looked up from where he was reclining, half in and half out of his old doghouse.

"Were you whining, Dagney?" asked Candie.

Dagney put his head back down on his paws. He loved Candie. He always had. But he didn't feel like romping or playing as much as he once had.

"If you ask me," Dagney thought, "napping the day away is far more delightful."

But who could nap with that incessant chirping noise going on next to his old doghouse? Dagney looked over toward the noise.

"What is it, boy?" Candie asked him gently. "What are you looking at?"

Dagney put his head down again and wondered some more about the sound. Candie curled up on the grass next to Dagney and stroked his head between his ears just the way he liked it. As the two of them, aging canine and young girl, sat together, Candie heard a chirping noise in the tall grass near Dagney's old doghouse.

"Oh, Dagney, do you hear that sound?" Candie exclaimed. "It's so romantic!"

Romantic?! If Dagney could speak, he would have asked Candie if she'd gone daft. Candie didn't see the offended look on Dagney's face. She was busy remembering what she'd learned in science class.

"That chirping sound is called stridulation," she explained in her kindest voice. "It's the sound emitted by a male cricket's stridulatory organ—a large vein that runs along the bottom of each wing. Cricket wings have teeth like a comb. Some people think that crickets rub their legs together, but that's not true. The chirping happens when the male cricket rubs the top of one wing against the bottom of the other."

Dagney sighed. So this was romance. He was thinking that Candie may have been reading too many love stories, such as *Twilight*. Candie was always reading books.

"You're probably wondering what's so romantic about that, aren't you?" asked Candie. "Well, you see, male crickets have four different songs. They have a loud one for when they're calling to a female. A soft courting song is used when a female is close by. Male crickets emit a loud, aggressive song when the chemoreceptors on their antennae detect the presence of another male. And when crickets mate, the male produces a brief song."

Candie thought of something and began to giggle.

"I think the chirping we're hearing is a male cricket looking for a female. Hey! Maybe it's time for Cricket Prom! Hahahaha!"

Her laughter cheered him up. Candie was so smart, thought Dagney. He loved it when she taught him new things. Old dogs love learning new things.

But mostly old dogs love to have the spot between their ears stroked. Telling Dagney all about stridulation gave Candie a good reason to sit and stroke his head. Dagney decided that he liked the chirping sound after all.

Tale of a Tail

 GLENNIS WAS READING her book while lounging on the sunny beach. She loved the way her fluffy blue towel felt next to her warm skin. She stretched out her legs and wiggled her toes in the sand. Her pretty green, sparkly painted toenails glinted in the sunlight.

Glennis felt herself about to doze off several times. She was reading a new book and it was so good she kept shaking her head to try to stay awake. As the afternoon wore on, her eyelids became so heavy she decided to shut them just for a moment.

"I'll rest my eyes for a minute or so," she thought.

Meanwhile, the tide was coming in. After a short while the water's edge reached Glennis's beach towel. She moved her feet off to the side but that only helped for a minute. After a few more ebbs and flows of the tide, the ocean tickled her toes, swishing her pretty green, sparkly painted toenails with cool water.

Glennis began to feel a strange sensation in her legs. All at once they became cold and clammy, then warm and tingly. Swiftly, Glennis looked down. She couldn't believe her eyes. Glennis no longer had legs or feet or toes with pretty toenails. Instead she had a green, shimmering tail!

Glennis looked around the shore. Moments ago the beach had been full of people, but now there wasn't a soul in sight.

Glennis was still in shock about having a tail, but she didn't have time to think about that. She had the urge to swim and the urge was overpowering. With the ocean right in front of her, she could satisfy her urge. Like the day she was starving and had a Nutella waffle placed in front of her. Or the day she was hot and thirsty and her mother gave her a giant glass of icy lemonade with a blue straw.

Glennis slipped into the water. Instantly she felt more freedom than she'd ever felt in her life.

After a while, Glennis began to feel more confident and courageous in the water. She moved farther from the shore and dove deeper into the sea. She noticed some charming little schools of fish. She was able to see them close up and from angles she'd never seen before, even when she'd been snorkeling with her dad. Glennis was able to closely examine and admire many exquisite rocks, majestic reefs, and the seaweed beds that frolicked in the tide.

Dandelion Wishes

Glennis loved the feel of the water rushing almost through her as she swam at a pace that was not possible with legs and feet.

Suddenly, she heard a nearby splash. Glennis looked around, shielding the bright sun from her eyes with one hand while she used her enchanting tail and the other hand to tread water.

About ten feet away was the most darling little gray dolphin! He swam slowly up to Glennis, his little dolphin mouth smiling the way that they do. Glennis smiled back. With a bob of his head, the dolphin motioned to her to follow him.

For quite some time, Glennis and the dolphin swam side by side. Occasionally, one or the other would jump or splash. It was great fun!

Eventually, Glennis decided to swim back to the spot on the beach where she had left her towel. She blew a kiss to the dolphin and waved goodbye. She thought it would be wise to get her cell phone out of her beach bag. She wanted to call her family and let them know she was staying longer at the beach. She didn't want them to worry.

"Should I tell them about my tail?" she wondered as she swam.

Soon she spotted her cottony blue towel. Scooping sand with her hands and thrusting with her tail, she made her way to the towel. But crawling along in the sand was making her tired.

"I'll rest my eyes for a minute or so," she thought.

After what seemed like only the briefest moment, she opened her eyes. Glennis looked down to check her new tail. Instead, she saw her pretty green, sparkly painted toenails.

Shell Conscious

 PENELOPE'S NICKNAME WAS PEBBLES. Her best friend's name was Sandra, but everyone called her Sandy. They had lived on the beach for so long they were part of it, really.

Every morning the cold and frothy water lapped over them until they were bathed awake. The girls then tumbled side by side through the waves. They agreed it was a wonderful life.

Sometimes Herman (Hermie for short) lugged his shell to where Pebbles and Sandy were sunbathing to say hello.

One fine day in the month of August, Pebbles, Sandy, Hermie and his friend Dungeness (Nessie for short) were playing jump rope with a bit of seaweed. It was a funny sight because none of them were very good at it. Crabs mostly crawl and tiny rocks mostly loll about in the sand, but they made a good effort and were having a lot of fun.

Suddenly, Shelly and Conch washed up nearby.

"Oh, look," said Shelly, "they're playing the games we used to play in elementary school!"

"How weird!" Conch chortled.

Pebbles and Sandy felt awkward being teased about playing jump rope and they stopped jumping.

Hermie saw their sad faces and said, "Don't feel self-conscious!" But just then a wave washed up and he got a mouthful of salt water. It sounded like Hermie said, "Don't feel shell-conscious!"

Nessie said, "Now, that was a funny coincidence—not!"

"What do you mean?" Pebbles and Sandy asked in unison.

Nessie replied, "When the seashells were making fun of us, instead of saying 'Don't feel self-conscious,' Hermie said, 'Don't feel shell-conscious'!"

This made Pebbles, Sandy, Hermie and Nessie break out into giggles. They decided to take Hermie's advice and happily returned to playing jump rope.

"Oh, look," said Shelly. "They're playing little baby games again!"

"Yeah," said Conch. "They're jumping around like they've got ants in their pants."

"Or sand in their eyes!" Shelly said, feeling very clever.

Shelly and Conch watched to see what their teasing would do. When they noticed it was having no effect on the little rocks and sand crabs, they were grumpy.

"They're no fun," said Shelly.

"Yeah, they can't take a joke!" said Conch.

Pebbles, Sandy, Hermie and Nessie were laughing about the seaweed jump rope getting caught in Hermie's claw and didn't even hear the latest teasing.

"Let's go," said Shelly.

"Yeah, let's find some sand fleas to bug," said Conch.

Shelly and Conch headed down the beach. When the seashells moved on, the four jump rope friends were having so much fun, they didn't even notice.

Star Power

 ONCE UPON A TIME in a galaxy far far away, there was a tiny little star. She was possibly the smallest star ever. Her name was Celeste.

Celeste was not popular with the other stars in the galaxy. She shone very bright for her size, but still the other stars ignored her.

"They're just jealous of your beauty," her mother told her.

Some simply judged her because of her size.

One lovely winter evening it was snowing down on Earth. It was cold because of the snow, and dark because the moon was but a waning crescent that night. Celeste looked down and saw a tiny little brindle dog walking through the snow. It seemed to be lost!

Celeste called to the other stars to come out and help light the way for the little brindle dog so he could find his way home.

"It's too cold," said one of the stars.

"I'm staying in the clouds where it's warmer," said another.

Celeste was brave and caring. She summoned all of her spirit and energy. She closed her eyes and began to glow. With each passing moment Celeste's little body got brighter and brighter. Soon the whole night sky was awash with shimmering starlight.

The little brindle dog's tail began to wag. Now he was able to see the road home! He scampered down the path, barking happily, and wagging his tail.

The other stars peeked out to see what all the commotion was about. They couldn't believe their eyes. *It was Celeste!* And she was lighting up the way for the cutest little brindle dog to find his way home in the snow. They were in awe of her bravery and beauty.

"Celeste!" the other stars said in unison. "We're so impressed with you!"

"Thank you," said Celeste, who was never one to hold a grudge.

"Would you like to come hang out with us?" said the other stars. "We're singing 'Twinkle, Twinkle, Little Star.'"

"Sure," said Celeste. "Just as soon as the little brindle dog gets home safely."

– The End –

If you enjoyed *Dandelion Wishes*,

please leave a review for the author on the website

where you purchased the book.

Subscribe to news from author Cheri Wood at

cheriwood.com

Follow Cheri on Facebook:

facebook.com/cheriwoodauthor

Follow Cheri on Twitter:

@cheriwoodbooks

About the author

Cheri Wood has three daughters, two grandchildren (so far), and three granddogs (so far). She loves to write, but her deep love is service work, especially with children. She has been a Girl Scout leader, a classroom volunteer, and has served on parent associations or advisory boards of all the schools her children have attended. A litigation attorney turned mediator, Cheri is an active member of her church and works with a nonprofit organization that advocates for transgender youth. She loves travel, movies, hiking, and Adam Lambert. Cheri lives in sunny Southern California where she enjoys the beach, mountains, and desert.

cheriwood.com
author@cheriwood.com